Pony-Crazed Princess

Princess Ellie's Camping Trip

Read all the adventures of Princess Ellie!

#1 Princess Ellie to the Rescue

#2 Princess Ellie's Secret

#3 Princess Ellie's Mystery

#4 Princess Ellie's Starlight Adventure

#5 Princess Ellie's Camping Trip

Pony-Crazed Princess

Princess Ellie's Camping Trip

by Diana Kimpton

Illustrated by Lizzie Finlay

Hyperion Paperbacks for Children

New York

For Rebecca

First published in the United Kingdom in 2004 as
The Pony-Mad Princess: Princess Ellie's Moonlight Mystery
by Usborne Publishing Ltd.
Based on an original concept by Anne Finnis
Text copyright © 2004 by Diana Kimpton and Anne Finnis
Illustrations copyright © 2004 by Lizzie Finlay

Printed in the United States of America
First U.S. edition, 2006
1 3 5 7 9 10 8 6 4 2

This book is set in 14.5-point Nadine Normal.
ISBN 0-7868-4874-X
Visit www.hyperionbooksforchildren.com

Chapter 1

"They said yes!" yelled Princess Ellie as she ran into the yard. Her frilly pink dress looked ridiculous with her Wellington boots. But she didn't care. She was in too much of a hurry to share her good news.

"That's terrific," said her best friend, Kate. She bounced up and down with excitement, sending the water slopping over the edge of the bucket she was carrying.

Meg, the palace groom, put a bulging hay net beside Moonbeam's door. "I'm really happy for you. But I must admit I'm surprised. I didn't think the King and Queen would approve of your going camping."

"Neither did I," said Kate. She put the bucket beside the hay net and undid the bolt on the door. Moonbeam poked her head out to see what was happening. She spotted Ellie immediately and whinnied a welcome.

Ellie grinned and stroked the palomino's nose. "They didn't like the idea at first," she explained. "But the prime minister persuaded them it would do me some good. We'll be perfectly safe on the palace grounds, and he thinks it will be character-forming, whatever that means."

"I think it'll be fun," laughed Kate as she

swung Moonbeam's door open and carried the bucket inside.

"So do I," said Ellie. She picked up the hay net and followed her friend into the stall.

Moonbeam immediately started pulling out pieces of hay. She made the net bounce and jiggle so much that it was hard for Ellie to tie it to the ring on the wall.

Kate pushed the hungry pony away so that Ellie could finish quickly. Then she grabbed Ellie by the arm and pulled her impatiently toward the door. "Come on," she said. "I've got something really exciting to show you."

"Can't it wait?" asked Ellie. "We've got so much to plan."

"There's loads of time to do that," replied Kate. "You've got to see this first."

Ellie was intrigued. What could be more exciting than planning their camping trip? She followed her friend around the back of the palace, past the garages and storerooms, until they reached the workshop. Kate's grandfather was waiting for them there. He was the palace handyman, and this was his special place.

As soon as he opened the door, Ellie saw what the secret was. Two tiny lambs tottered toward them, bleating loudly. "They're so cute!" she said, as she kneeled down on the dusty floor. One came closer and sucked one of her fingers.

"They're hungry," said Kate's grandfather. "You're just in time to give them these." He handed each of the girls a feeding bottle full of warm milk.

The lambs immediately started to suck hungrily. Ellie was surprised at how hard they pulled on the bottle to get the milk. She had to hold her bottle tightly to stop it

from being tugged right out of her hands.

"Why do you have them?" she asked. "I thought the shepherd at the farm looked after all the sheep."

"He does," laughed Kate's grandfather. "And they keep him very busy. That's why I'm giving him a hand with these two."

"Grandpa's great with animals," explained Kate. "He's reared loads of lambs before— and some kittens, and even a deer."

Kate's grandfather smiled. "His name was

Stanley," he explained. "I found him when he was a tiny fawn. He must have been in an accident; he'd been badly hurt."

"Grandpa nursed him back to health," added Kate, who had obviously heard the story many times before.

"Not quite," said her grandfather. "His left ear was never the same again. It drooped sideways and made him look a little different. Which he was, of course. He's not timid like a normal deer."

"What happened to him?" asked Ellie. "Did you keep him as a pet?"

The old man shook his head. "You can't keep a wild animal cooped up. It isn't right. When he was big enough, I let him go free in the deer park." He stared out of the window and smiled. "That was over two years ago now, but I still see him sometimes when I'm out there doing some work."

Ellie fed the last few drops of milk to the lamb. It was sleepy now that its stomach was full, so she cradled it in her arms, delighting in the soft warmth of its body. "My parents said we could go camping," she announced proudly. "We're going to take two of my ponies with us. I got the idea from one of my books."

"It's going to be a lot of fun," said Kate. "Two whole nights away from home."

"Two whole nights of total freedom," added Ellie, with such enthusiasm that the lamb woke up. "No rules, no governess, no nothing."

Kate's grandfather smiled and raised his eyebrows. "And you both know all about the ins and outs of camping, do you?"

Ellie hesitated. There was something in his voice that suggested he didn't think they did. But she'd read a book about it. She must know enough, she thought. "I'm going to talk to my father about the arrangements later," she said confidently.

"Then we'd better start planning," said Kate. She pulled some paper and a pencil from a shelf and started to make a list of equipment. "I know what we need, because I've been camping lots of times with Mom and Dad." Kate's dad traveled a lot, because he built roads and bridges for a living. Kate stayed with her grandparents so she

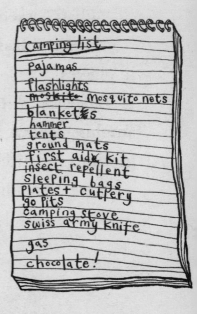

Camping list

Pajamas
flashlights
moskito mosquito nets
blankets
hammer
tents
ground mats
first aid kit
insect repellent
sleeping bags
plates + cutlery
go pits
camping stove
swiss army knife

gas
chocolate!

didn't have to keep changing schools.

"But that was in other places," said Ellie. "The palace grounds are different. They're not like the jungle, or the desert."

"That's true," agreed Kate, crossing "mosquito nets" off the list. "But we still need tents, and sleeping bags, and go pits."

"What pits?" asked Ellie.

"Go pits," said Kate. "They're holes in the ground. For, you know . . ."

"What?" asked Ellie in confusion.

"Toilets," hissed Kate, before collapsing in giggles.

Ellie gulped. Her book hadn't mentioned anything about that. Maybe camping was going to be harder than she'd expected.

Chapter 2

By the time they had finished their planning, Ellie was late for meeting her father. She raced back to the palace at top speed and burst into his office, immediately handling him her list of equipment. Then she stopped in dismay. Sitting next to the King was Ellie's governess, Miss Stringle. They were both staring at her in disapproval.

"Just look at the state of your clothes,

Aurelia," said the King. "You're a mess."

Ellie winced at the sound of her real name, but she knew he was right. Her pink dress was covered with a mixture of dust from the workshop and dribbles of milk. There were pieces of hay stuck to the ruffles, and several of the ribbon bows had come undone. "I'm sorry," she said, as convincingly as she could. "I've been busy feeding a lamb and making plans for the camping trip."

The King sighed and glanced at his watch. "There's no time for you to get changed now. Anyway, I'm due in another meeting soon, so

I've asked Miss Stringle to help make the arrangements."

Ellie groaned inwardly. This could take all the fun out of camping. Her governess had strict ideas on how princesses should behave.

Miss Stringle stood up and leafed through the pile of papers she was holding. Then she coughed politely, curtsied to the King, and announced, "I estimate that we'll need eight tents."

"Eight! What for?" asked Ellie. "We only need two—one for me and Kate and one for the ponies."

"Nonsense," declared Miss Stringle. "You're a princess. You can't possibly share a tent with someone who isn't royal."

Ellie glared at her angrily. "But Kate's my

best friend," she argued. "I'd be lonely without her."

"That's a very good point," said the King. "And it would mean one less tent. So who are the others for?"

Miss Stringle counted on her fingers as she reeled off the names. "There's Princess Aurelia's personal maid, to tidy her tent; a cook to prepare the food; a footman to serve the meals; a groom to care for the ponies . . ."

"No, no, no," Ellie interrupted. "Camping is about freedom and doing everything ourselves. We don't need servants, and we definitely don't need a groom. Kate and I can look after the ponies ourselves."

". . . And another maid, to wash the dishes," continued Miss Stringle, taking no notice of the interruption.

"We don't need her, either," said Ellie, in a voice too loud to ignore. She had never washed dishes in her life, but she was determined to make her own rules for the camping trip.

The King took the list from Miss Stringle and read it thoughtfully. "I admire you for wanting to do everything the hard way," he told Ellie, with a mischievous glint in his eye, "so you obviously won't want this portable toilet that Miss Stringle has mistakenly ordered." He picked up a pencil and began to cross the offending item off the list.

Thoughts of go pits rushed through

Ellie's mind, and she leaped forward to stop him. "You can leave that if you like."

The King smiled. "That's good to hear. Now, let's see if we can work out some other compromises."

Miss Stringle stared at her list thoughtfully. "I suppose we could do without the second maid if we tell the footman to wash up."

"No," said Ellie. "We want to do it all."

"But you can't possibly put the tents up yourselves," argued Miss Stringle. "They're much too heavy for a princess to carry."

"Okay," Ellie agreed reluctantly. "I don't mind someone else doing that. But only if they go home afterward."

"That seems reasonable enough," agreed the King.

"But you're not doing any cooking," insisted Miss Stringle. "That would be much too undignified for a princess, and it would be unsafe. I will arrange for all your meals to be sent up from the palace."

"Can't we at least make our own breakfast?" pleaded Ellie. "That's not difficult."

"You can take cereal and milk," said the King. "But I agree with Miss Stringle about the danger of fires. We'll send up the hot water for bathing."

"We won't need that," said Ellie. "The children in my book fetched their water from the stream, and we're going to do the same."

The King looked at her doubtfully. "If

that's what you want . . . But I don't think you're going to enjoy camping as much as you think."

"Neither do I, Your Majesty," agreed Miss Stringle. "It's really not a suitable activity for a princess."

"Yes, it is," said Ellie. "I'm going to be away for a whole weekend, and I'm going to love every minute of it."

"If you don't, you can always come back early," sighed the King. "I'm sure you won't last two whole nights in a tent."

Ellie glared at him. She was sure he was wrong. He must be. How could freedom not be fun?

Chapter 3

Ellie's excitement increased as the week went on. She found it even harder than usual to concentrate on her lessons. She couldn't think of anything but the camping trip.

It was easy to decide which ponies to take. Moonbeam and Rainbow were the obvious choices. Shadow, the Shetland, was too small; Sundance was too good at escaping; and Starlight, the newest arrival, wasn't fit enough to be ridden very much yet.

Choosing a campsite was more difficult. Miss Stringle wanted it to be close to the palace, while Ellie wanted it as far away as possible. Neither of them would change her mind until Meg discovered the perfect spot—a pretty clearing in the woods on the other side of the deer park. Ellie and Kate fell in love with the dazzling sunshine and the babbling stream as soon as they saw the campsite, and even Miss Stringle had to agree it was a good choice. It was far enough from the palace to be private, but close enough for the food still to be hot when it arrived.

At long last, Friday came. The last royal waving lesson of the week was over, and it was time to set out for the campsite. Ellie and Kate mounted Moonbeam and Rainbow, and everyone came to see them off. Even the servants leaned out of the palace windows to wave good-bye.

Meg gave the girls a large envelope containing directions for a treasure hunt to keep them busy on Saturday. Kate's grandmother, the palace cook, gave them food for midnight snacks. Miss Stringle also gave them something: a gift-wrapped package.

"Pencils and paper," she explained. "In case you want to write an essay while you're away."

"Is she serious?" whispered Kate.

"Yes, she is," replied Ellie, pushing the unopened package toward the bottom of her backpack. "She's a teacher. She always wants to spoil everything by making me write about it."

The King and Queen were the last to say their farewells. They had both put on their second-best crowns, to mark the importance of the occasion. The Queen looked worried as she kissed Ellie good-bye. "I hope you enjoy it," she said.

"But I don't expect you will," added the King. He handed Ellie a cell phone in a red-velvet case embroidered with the royal crest. "Call us when you've had enough, and we'll send someone to bring you home."

"I won't need it," declared Ellie. She put the phone into her backpack, tucking it firmly under Miss Stringle's package. "This is going to be the best weekend of my whole life. I'll see you on Sunday, when we get back."

Moonbeam seemed to share Ellie's excitement and eagerness to be on the move. She tossed her head as Ellie shortened the reins, her snow-white mane cascading in all directions.

"This is going to be fantastic," said Kate, as she rode up beside Ellie on Rainbow.

After one last wave at everyone, they

trotted out of the stable yard and away from the palace. It was a path they often took when they went for a ride. But today it felt different. Today it was leading them to an adventure.

As they turned in to the deer park, Ellie looked back. The Queen was still there, waving her handkerchief. For the first time, Ellie realized how strange it was going to be at bedtime, when there was no one to kiss her good night. But she pushed the thought away and concentrated on the pleasure of riding.

Although the girls were eager to

reach the campsite, they decided not to go there by the shortest route. Riding the long way would make it feel further away and more like an adventure. It would also let the ponies burn off their surplus energy before they all settled down for the night.

They cantered along the edge of the deer park. Then they slowed to a walk and turned on to a path that zigzagged its way up the hillside. It was so narrow that the ferns on either side swished against their legs. Moonbeam grabbed some as she went past. The leaves were too big to fit in her mouth, so they hung out either side.

"You're nearly as greedy as Shadow," laughed Ellie, leaning forward and pulling the leaves out from between the pony's teeth.

The path grew wider when they reached the wood, so they started to trot. Rays of sunlight shone between the branches; the ponies' hooves made hardly any sound on the soft ground. Ellie's excitement grew and grew as each step took them closer to the campsite.

At long last, they reached the edge of the trees and rode out into the sunshine. They stopped and stared in surprise.

"Wow!" said Kate. "I've never seen a tent like that before."

Neither had Ellie. The tent on the front of her book had been made of plain green canvas. This one was neither plain nor green. It was bright pink and decorated with gold bows and embroidered gold crowns. Miniature versions of the royal flag fluttered at each end. Even the ropes that held the tent up were made of golden cord.

"I'm sorry," laughed Ellie. "Miss Stringle never mentioned this."

Fortunately, her governess had left the rest of the arrangements to Meg, so the pony shelter was made of simple white canvas. It was large and airy, with a roof to protect Moonbeam and Rainbow from the rain, and three sides to protect them from the wind. The fourth side was open, to make sure they got plenty of light.

Ellie felt very proud as she led Moonbeam inside. It was the first time she and Kate had ever been completely responsible for the ponies. They quickly unsaddled them, put on their halters, and tied them to the rope that ran along the back of the shelter. They left the ponies munching on some hay while they went to get water.

The girls couldn't resist exploring the pink tent first. The inside was nearly as grand as the outside. The roof was lined with gold silk and embroidered with silver stars. There was a pink-satin ribbon wrapped around the tent poles, and the floor was covered with a pink carpet.

To Ellie's relief, Miss Stringle had remembered that she wanted to sleep on the ground. So there were no four-poster camp beds, just two sleeping bags—one on each side of the tent. On a small table at the far end stood a box of cereal and a container of milk for breakfast in the morning.

The most exciting thing of all was that there was no adult in sight. The girls really were free to do as they pleased. "This is so much fun," said Ellie, as she picked up her bucket and headed for the stream.

Even collecting the water was much more

exciting than using a tap. The stream bub-
bled over rocks and down a tiny waterfall
into a wide, shallow pool with stepping
stones arranged in a row across it. It was such
a fun place to play that they stayed much
longer than they needed to.

The sun was low in the sky by the time
they carried their full buckets back to the
campsite.

The tents looked peaceful in the evening sunset. But as soon as the girls reached the pony shelter, they realized that something was terribly wrong. Moonbeam's halter was still tied to the rope, but Moonbeam wasn't in it anymore. The palomino pony had disappeared.

Chapter 4

Ellie looked around desperately, but there was no sign of Moonbeam. She bent down and picked up the empty halter. "It's still fastened. She must have wriggled it over her ears."

"Do you think she's gone home?" asked Kate.

"I hope not," groaned Ellie. "Everyone will laugh at us if she has."

Suddenly there was a noise coming from the bright pink tent. Ellie and Kate raced over and lifted the door flap. Inside, they saw a snow-white tail. And there was Moonbeam, with her head deep inside the box of cereal as she happily munched on its contents.

"That's our breakfast!" shouted Kate.

"She'll have our midnight snack, too, if we don't get her out soon," said Ellie. She tried to squeeze past Moonbeam's backside and into the tent. But the pony whisked her tail and raised a hoof in warning.

"Watch out in case she kicks!" called Kate.

"I forgot that ponies don't like to be disturbed while they're eating," said Ellie, quickly backing out of the tent.

"But we can't just leave her till she's finished," said Kate.

The obvious solution was to find another way in. But a quick search soon revealed that there wasn't one. Miss Stringle had thought of everything they might need, except a back door. Ellie tried a different approach.

"Good girl," called Ellie in a soothing voice, as she braced herself for a second attempt at rescuing their supplies. The palomino pony stopped munching and listened. Squeezing past, Ellie put a reassuring hand on Moonbeam's rump and said, "It's only me." The pony flicked her ears and whisked her tail again, but she didn't kick.

Ellie moved quickly along Moonbeam's

side and grabbed hold of her mane. Then she put the halter around the pony's neck to stop her from escaping as she tried to pull her head out of the cereal box.

Moonbeam didn't make it easy. She was determined to eat as much as possible while she had the chance. She stepped sideways, trying to push Ellie away. In the process, her hoof landed on the container of milk, crushing it completely and spraying milk in all directions.

Ellie grabbed hold of the cereal box with her free hand and pulled so hard that it tore open. Golden flakes spilled down to join the puddle of milk on the floor. Moonbeam pushed her head down to try to eat them, but Ellie was too quick for her. She slipped the halter on and buckled it in place.

"Now we just have to get her outside," said Ellie.

Kate peered in through the entrance. "I don't think there's room to turn her around," she groaned.

"Can we get her out backward?" asked Ellie.

Kate looked doubtful. "Only if she goes absolutely straight."

Ellie sighed. "We'll have to try. There's no other way." She started to coax Moonbeam to walk backward. The pony reluctantly obeyed. She was still trying to reach the last of the cereal.

"Careful," called Kate. "She's swinging to the left."

Ellie tried again. One step. Two steps . . .

Suddenly, Moonbeam's back foot landed

on an umbrella that Miss Stringle had provided. It triggered the release button, and the umbrella unfolded with a loud whoosh.

The sudden movement terrified Moonbeam. Before Ellie could stop her, the pony lurched forward, charged into the back wall of the tent, and swung around.

Kate was right. There wasn't room in the tent for Moonbeam to turn. Her hindquarters smashed into the rear tent pole, cracking it in two. The top half of the pole crashed down, hitting the pony as it fell. The shock sent Moonbeam into an even greater panic. As the roof of the tent collapsed around her, she hurtled for the entrance.

Luckily, this time she got through. Ellie tore after her, half running and half being dragged along, clinging desperately to the

rope. She was determined not to let
Moonbeam disappear again.

Moonbeam finally stopped at the edge of
the clearing. Ellie and Kate stroked her face
and spoke to her soothingly until she settled
down and started to graze.

Then they looked at the tent in dismay. It
was a total disaster. One end had collapsed

completely, so that the roof was lying on the ground. The other end was still vaguely upright, but it wouldn't take much of a wind to bring it down. There was no way they could sleep in it in that condition.

Chapter 5

"I don't want to go home," wailed Kate as they tied Moonbeam up in the pony shelter, making sure her halter was secure this time.

"Neither do I," sighed Ellie. Most of all, she didn't want to call her father and admit that something had already gone wrong. The thought of the King's saying, "I told you so," filled her with fresh determination. "It's only a broken pole. We must be able to fix that."

They went back to the damaged tent and
crawled inside. Ellie struggled to her feet,
lifting the collapsed roof high above her
head.

"That's better," laughed Kate.
"If you can just stand there for the
next two days, everything will be
fine."

"Don't be silly," giggled Ellie.

"Just grab the pieces of pole and bring them outside." She held up the roof until Kate had safely exited the tent. Then she let go and ran outside as the tent collapsed again.

They detached the pink ribbon from the pole and used it to tie the broken pieces together. It didn't work. The join was so wobbly that they had to undo it all and start again.

Suddenly, Ellie had an idea. She looked inside her backpack and pulled out the unopened package from Miss Stringle. "Maybe this is going to be more useful than we thought," said Ellie as she unwrapped it. Inside were the sheets of

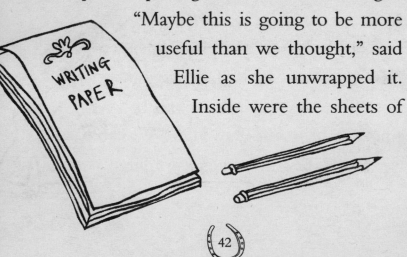

paper and two pencils that Miss Stringle had packed. Ellie pulled the paper out and wrapped it tightly around the join in the pole.

She placed the pencils on either side to act as a splint, added a layer of brightly colored wrapping paper, and tied everything together with the ribbon. This time, the join didn't wobble.

Back in the tent, Ellie lifted up the roof again, as Kate carefully eased the pole into position. Then Ellie let go, and they both held their breath as the pole took the full weight of the tent.

"Yippee!" cried Kate. The mended pole stood straight and tall. Their repair had worked.

"We're brilliant," said Ellie. "We can handle anything."

Their celebration was cut short by the sound of a car's engine. They ran outside just in time to see the royal Range Rover arrive.

Higginbottom, the butler, stepped down from the driver's seat and bowed. "His Majesty asked me to check to see if everything was all right, Your Highness." He looked completely out of place in his evening suit and white gloves.

"Everything's fine," Ellie replied quickly. She crossed her fingers behind her back, hoping he wouldn't notice that the tent looked a little different than it had when he'd put it up. Several of the gold bows had come undone in the chaos, and one of the royal flags had fallen off completely.

To Ellie's relief, he didn't seem to notice. Neither did the footmen, who were unloading huge silver trays with matching covers.

"Dinner!" cried Ellie with delight. Her tummy felt so empty that she was tempted to start eating immediately. But she didn't. She waited until Higginbottom had driven away. She didn't want her feeling of freedom being spoiled by having servants around.

Kate's grandmother obviously understood the needs of hungry campers. The trays held plates piled high with roast chicken, mashed potatoes, and lots of gravy.

By the time they had finished eating, the sun had set. They had to turn their flashlights on so they could see to eat their dessert.

Ellie was glad the food was hot. The warmth of the day had vanished with the sun, and she was feeling chilly. "Too bad we can't have a campfire," she said. "The children in my book all sit around a fire and sing songs after dinner."

"We can still sing," suggested Kate. "We did that every night when I camped in the desert with my mom and dad." She paused as a large raindrop landed on her nose, then added, "But it didn't rain there."

Ellie watched in dismay as more drops splashed into her pudding bowl. "It didn't rain in my book, either," she grumbled.

Then the clouds burst, releasing a deluge. The girls rushed into the tent and gazed out, waiting for it to stop. But it didn't. Instead, it settled into a steady downpour that was obviously going to last for a while.

The gloomy weather made the girls feel gloomy, too. Neither of them felt like singing anymore. "Let's go to bed," Ellie suggested. "Maybe it'll be better in the morning."

But even going to bed was harder than she had expected. First, there was the run through the rain and darkness to the portable toilet. Then there was another wet run to the pony shelter, to check on Moonbeam and Rainbow.

Finally, there was the problem of the nightgown. Kate was lucky; she didn't have one. Instead, she had sensible pony-print pajamas. But Ellie had a ridiculously frilly pink nightgown made for a princess in a four-poster bed. It was definitely not designed for wearing in a sleeping bag. Ellie slid her feet into her sleeping bag and tried to shimmy down inside it. But the nightgown refused to slide down with her. She ended up with it wrapped around her neck like a scarf. She crawled out and tried again. The same thing happened.

On her third attempt, she gripped the hem of the nightgown tightly between her knees. This made sliding somewhat tricky, but it worked. Finally, both Ellie and the nightgown were inside the sleeping bag. By then, Kate was already curled up snugly in hers, nearly asleep.

"Good night," whispered Ellie, as she switched off her flashlight. Night seemed much darker in the tent than it did at the palace. It was certainly colder, and definitely damper.

Ellie wriggled around trying to get comfortable on the hard ground. Perhaps she shouldn't have turned down the camp bed that Miss Stringle had offered. At this rate, she was going to be awake all night.

But eventually the pitter-patter of the rain on the tent acted like a lullaby, and she drifted off to sleep.

She woke up suddenly. For a moment,

she wondered where she was. Then she heard the sound that had awakened her. Ellie's eyes snapped wide open in fear. There was something outside—something that was shuffling along the edge of the tent, trying to get in!

Chapter 6

Ellie felt her heart start to race as the shuffling grew closer and closer. Now the creature was just on the other side of the tent wall, only a few inches from her head. She froze, remembering scary stories of wild wolves.

Then she thought of Moonbeam and relaxed. The pony must have escaped again and come looking for more cereal. Ellie just needed to go outside and get her. Then the noise would stop.

But then, suddenly, something scratched at the tent wall—something like a claw. There was no way a pony could make a sound like that. It couldn't be Moonbeam.

It must be a wolf.

Ellie fumbled for her flashlight. Maybe bright light would drive the creature away. But in her panic, she knocked the flashlight over, and it tumbled with a loud clang into a container of hoof oil. Instantly, the shuffling stopped, and a moment later, Ellie heard something crash through the bushes.

Kate sat bolt upright in her sleeping bag. "What's going on?" she asked, snapping her flashlight on.

"There's something outside," whispered Ellie. "I heard it shuffling near the tent. It was trying to get in." She paused for a moment, before adding, "I think it was a wolf!"

Kate put her hands over her mouth in alarm and shrank down as if somehow being smaller would make her safer. They sat very still and listened. The only sound they heard was their own breathing. Even the rain had died down.

"I don't hear anything," whispered Kate.

"Neither do I," Ellie whispered back. "Maybe it ran away."

"Unless you dreamed it," suggested Kate.

"I didn't!" declared Ellie. "I was as awake as I am now, and I promise you there was something just outside the tent."

"But it couldn't have been a wolf," said Kate. "There aren't any wolves on the palace grounds."

"That's what everyone thinks," explained Ellie. "But just because nobody's seen one doesn't mean there aren't any here."

"That's true," said Kate. She shivered with fear, pulling the sleeping bag up to her chin. Then she dropped it again suddenly as her eyes opened wide with horror. "What about the ponies? What if the wolf's gone after them?"

Neither of them wanted to go outside. But their love for Moonbeam and Rainbow overcame their fear. They crept out to the pony shelter, holding hands to give each other courage. Kate carried the flashlight.

Ellie was armed with the remains of the umbrella.

She didn't need it. There was no sign of the wolf, and the shelter looked exactly as it had when they had gone to sleep. Moonbeam and Rainbow turned their heads to see who was disturbing their sleep. Their eyes glittered in the bright beam of the flashlight.

Ellie hugged Moonbeam and pressed her face close to the pony's neck. The warm smell of horse was reassuring; it reminded her of home. "Perhaps we could bring our sleeping bags over here to sleep," she said.

Kate shook her head. "There's not enough room. We'd end up being trampled."

They lingered for as long as they could, stroking the ponies and rearranging their hay. But the cold soon seeped through their thin pajamas and attacked their toes inside their boots. After a while they were shivering so much that they had to run back to the tent to get warm.

Kate dived into her sleeping bag and pulled it tight around her neck. "I suppose we could eat something," she suggested.

Ellie didn't reply right away. She was too

busy struggling with her nightgown as she wriggled into her bag. But once she was inside, she opened her backpack and pulled out the food Kate's grandmother had packed for them.

Nestled underneath the food was the phone the King had given her. Ellie bit her lip nervously as she stared at it. All she had to do was make one call and they'd be whisked back to the safety and warmth of the palace. But that would mean admitting that her father had been right—that she couldn't cope with the freedom of being on her own.

Ellie closed the backpack again and pushed it away. She passed Kate a bar of chocolate and kept one for herself.

This wasn't how she had imagined their midnight snack. She had pictured them sitting out under the stars feeling happy, not curled up in their sleeping bags, cold and scared.

They ate in silence, listening for any more strange sounds. The creamy chocolate helped them feel better. When they'd finished, they settled down to sleep again. Neither of them wanted to creep out into the darkness to brush their teeth.

"They won't go rotten in one night," declared Kate.

Ellie happily agreed. But when she lay down to sleep, the silence seemed scarier, the night darker, and the ground even harder than before. She tossed and turned for what seemed like forever. But eventually she dozed off.

When she woke up, sunlight was streaming into the tent. It made everything look warm and friendly again and drove away her fear. She was tired after her sleepless night, and so was Kate. Reluctantly, they crawled out of their sleeping bags and threw on clean clothes.

Ellie was glad they'd gotten some water the night before. She didn't feel like walking to the stream that early in the morning. But as soon as she put her finger in the bucket, she pulled it right out again. "It's freezing," she said. "Do you want to wash up first?"

Kate felt the water and shook her head. "I don't think I want to wash up at all. We aren't very dirty, are we?"

Ellie had a feeling they were, but she wasn't going to argue. She was too busy regretting turning down the King's offer of hot water. "Let's see to the ponies before breakfast."

"What breakfast?" asked Kate. She picked up the remains of the cereal box and tipped out the few remaining flakes. "Thanks to your pony, we've got nothing to eat."

Ellie was feeling irritable after so little sleep. "What do you mean, *my* pony?" she snapped. "They're both my ponies—or have you forgotten?" She regretted the words as soon as she'd said them.

Kate's eyes filled with tears. "That's right. Rub it in. It's not my fault I don't have my own pony. My parents aren't rich like yours. Mine can't afford to buy me everything I want."

"I'm sorry," mumbled Ellie. But it was too late. The damage was done.

Kate turned away and stormed out of the tent.

Chapter 7

Ellie ran after her, determined to make things right. She found her in the pony shelter, crying into Rainbow's mane. As soon as Ellie arrived, Kate straightened up and wiped her tears away with her hands. Then she grabbed a dandy brush and began to groom the gray pony as if nothing were wrong.

Ellie followed her lead and started brushing Moonbeam. "Well, at least it's stopped raining," she said, in an attempt to lighten the mood.

Kate ignored her.

"And we can ride all day," Ellie continued.

Kate still said nothing.

"And I really am sorry," said Ellie, with much more sincerity than she had the first time. "I didn't mean to hurt your feelings."

Kate gave a silent shrug and concentrated on Rainbow's mane.

Ellie was nearly in tears herself. Kate was her best friend. They'd never argued before, and she wasn't sure she wanted to spend all day riding with someone who wouldn't speak to her. It was a relief when the Range Rover arrived.

Although it was morning, Higginbottom was once again wearing his evening suit. Ellie realized she had never seen him in anything else, and she wondered if he went to bed in it, too.

He bowed as he handed her two box lunches. Then he coughed politely and said in an embarrassed voice, "I know that is all you requested, Your Highness, but the cook refused to listen to me." He opened the back of the car and lifted the cover from one of the two silver trays inside. "She insisted I bring this, just in case, but I'm happy to take it back if you wish."

Ellie's mouth watered at the sight of sausages, bacon, eggs, and hot buttered toast. "You might as well leave it," she said, trying to hide her delight.

"It would be such a shame to see it go to waste," added Kate, peering over Ellie's shoulder. "And I wouldn't like to offend Grandma."

Ellie and Kate grinned at each other, and Ellie knew she was forgiven. They tore into their breakfast together. The hot food cheered them up and gave them the energy they needed to tackle the morning chores.

As they cleared away the manure and collected fresh water, they kept their eyes open for signs of the mysterious creature from the night before. But there weren't any. The short grass was too springy to show paw prints, and the snapped twig Ellie found beside the tent might have been there when they arrived.

By the time they set out on their ride, Ellie had nearly forgotten how frightened she had been during the night. It was wonderful to be back in the saddle and to have a whole day to enjoy with Kate. Moonbeam and Rainbow seemed as excited as their riders. They tossed their heads and kept trying to trot instead of walk.

Meg must have spent a long time planning the treasure hunt. When the girls opened the envelope she'd given them, they found a map with the route marked on it, questions about the places they would see on their way, and a list of birds and animals to look for as they went along.

"We have to spot a deer, a squirrel, a blackbird, a crow, a robin, and a pheasant," said Kate, examining the directions.

"And we start by going back the way we came yesterday," said Ellie, who was in charge of the map. She read the first question out loud: *"Through the wood to the giant pine, how many hollies stand in line?"*

"I remember that pine tree," squealed Kate. "Come on! Let's get started."

Soon, both girls were completely absorbed in the game. Meg had planned the route to make the riding fun. There were tiny paths to explore, small logs to jump, and wonderful long stretches of grass to canter across. And the questions were perfect, too—not too easy and not too difficult. The animal-spotting was the hardest part. All the creatures were well hidden and shy of visitors. It took sharp eyes and patience to find them.

Ellie felt completely happy as she rode along. This was how camping should be— just as it was in her book. If only it could always be that good. If only there hadn't been another night to get through; another night when the mysterious creature might come back to get them.

Chapter 8

It was late in the afternoon when Ellie and Kate rode down a wooded slope toward a wide stream.

"We're nearly finished," said Kate. "And we've only seen the birds so far."

"Don't worry," said Ellie. "There's still time." She pulled Moonbeam to a halt beside a fallen log and read the second-to-last clue on her sheet: *Find the log, and look up high. Whose home is that against the sky?"*

They peered up into the branches of the nearby tree, but all they saw was a tangle of twigs.

"What sort of bird lives there?" Kate wondered aloud.

Then a movement caught their eye. A red squirrel scampered into view. It sprang into another tree and disappeared behind the trunk.

"That's it," said Ellie triumphantly. "It's a squirrel's nest."

"Well, we can cross 'squirrel' off the list," added Kate. "So we've found everything now, except the deer."

"We might still see one," said Ellie.

Kate shook her head. "I think they're too

shy to come out into the open."

Ellie read the last clue. This one wasn't a question. It was an instruction: *"Across the stream and past the tree. Back to camp in time for tea.*

"That sounds like a good idea," she said with a yawn. "I'm tired, and the ponies must be, too." She urged Moonbeam into the stream they had to cross, but the palomino hesitated at the edge, peering nervously at the water.

"I'll go across first," said Kate. "Rainbow's hardly frightened of anything." She rode past Ellie, and the gray mare stepped happily into the stream.

"Come on, Moonbeam," said Ellie, as she and the palomino followed close behind.

The stream was deepest in the middle.

Rainbow decided to stop when the water got above her knees. Kate urged her on, but Rainbow took no notice. Instead, she started to paw at the water with a front hoof, sending cascades of droplets over her squealing rider.

"Stop it!" pleaded Kate.

Ellie giggled. "She thinks you should have bathed this morning."

Suddenly, Rainbow stopped splashing. But then she started to lie down in the water instead.

"No!" yelled Kate. She kicked the pony with her heels, but it made no difference.

Ellie tried to help. She rode up to Rainbow and leaned forward to try to grab the pony's bridle, but she couldn't reach it in time. The gray pony sank down into the stream with a sigh of satisfaction.

Kate jumped off and screamed as the ice-cold water soaked through her jodhpurs, and Ellie roared with laughter. It was the funniest sight she'd seen in a long time.

Suddenly, there was a crashing sound in the undergrowth beside the stream. Two terrified deer shot out of the bushes and

The noise frightened Moonbeam. She leaped sideways in an attempt to escape, and

the sudden movement took Ellie by surprise. She was still leaning forward and laughing so much that she wasn't paying attention to her own pony. Before she could steady herself, she lost her balance and slid over the palomino's shoulder. She landed flat on her back in the water with a huge splash.

Now it was Kate's turn to laugh. "Good! We've both had a bath. And we've finally seen a deer to complete the treasure hunt."

"I wonder what frightened them," said Ellie, as she struggled to her feet.

"Us laughing, I suppose," suggested Kate. Her face became more serious. "Unless . . ."

Ellie bit her lip nervously. "Are you thinking what I'm thinking?"

Kate nodded slowly.

"The wolf!" they both said at once.

Chapter 9

Ellie shivered as they rode quickly back to the campsite. The sun was too low in the sky to provide much warmth, and her wet clothes gave her no protection from the chilly breeze. But it wasn't just the cold that made her shiver. She was scared, too. The deer's fear had triggered her own, bringing back memories of last night's mysterious visitor.

As they reached the top of the hill, she caught a glimpse of the palace in the distance. It looked so warm and welcoming. She thought longingly of hot showers and soft, fluffy towels, but she didn't say anything. She didn't want Kate to think she was a wimp.

Their tent looked cold and unfriendly in comparison, but at least it would let them get out of the wind. They quickly unsaddled the ponies and gave them their hay. Then they ran to the pink tent to get changed. There was an awful odor inside. The spilled milk had gone bad in the warmth of the afternoon, and it smelled.

Kate wrinkled her nose in disgust as she struggled out of her wet jodhpurs. "That's what we get for not cleaning it up," she groaned.

Ellie had never even thought of cleaning up the milk, or picking up her dirty clothes, or straightening out her sleeping bag. No wonder her half of the tent was such a mess. She was so used to having servants around that she'd never realized how untidy she was.

She pulled off her wet clothes and dumped them in a reasonably tidy heap. Then she rubbed her arms and legs briskly with a towel to try to bring some warmth back into them. She was thankful that it was nearly dinnertime. Some hot food was just what she and Kate both needed.

Unfortunately, hot food wasn't what Higginbottom had brought. Kate's grandmother had provided chicken salad sandwiches and an icebox with two bowls of ice cream. She had probably thought it would be the ideal meal for the girls at the end of a sunny day.

"We would be much warmer at home," said Kate. She pulled her coat tightly around her as she sat on the grass nibbling her dinner. They didn't want to eat inside the smelly tent.

Ellie looked at her in surprise. "Are you feeling homesick, too?"

Kate nodded. "Just a little."

"But you should be fine. You've gone

camping lots of times," said Ellie.

"Not on my own," said Kate. "I've always had my mom and dad with me." She paused and looked nervously at the surrounding trees. "And there aren't any wolves in the desert."

Ellie knew exactly what she meant. The damp cold and the smelly tent were only part of the problem. Although she wasn't comfortable, she was sure she could cope if she tried hard enough. But wild animals with big teeth were another thing altogether. Surely her father wouldn't make fun of her for running away from a wolf.

"We could go home now if you wanted," she suggested. It wouldn't look so bad if Kate gave up first.

"No," replied her friend. "We'll be okay.

There's only one more night."

"And the wolf probably won't come back," added Ellie, with more confidence than she felt. Because it was so cold, she kept her coat on. She pulled the phone out of her backpack and slipped it into her coat pocket—just in case. If the mysterious visitor returned, she would call the palace right away.

When bedtime came, they rearranged the tent so that their sleeping bags were right next to each other. Then they put the ponies' saddlecloths over their pillows in the hope that the lovely horse smell would hide the disgusting smell of sour milk. They wriggled into their sleeping bags and huddled close together. But the ground was hard, and Ellie found it hard to fall asleep with her mind full of scary thoughts. She was still awake when the mystery visitor returned.

Ellie's stomach churned in fear as she listened to the shuffling. There was only a thin layer of tent separating her from the creature outside. Her imagination ran wild as she pictured sharp teeth and claws tearing at the fabric.

She reached over to awaken Kate, but she didn't need to. Her friend was already alert and listening. She took Ellie's hand and squeezed it reassuringly. At least they were both in this together.

The shuffling noises moved along the outside of the tent, finally reaching the doorway. Suddenly the sounds stopped, and the door flap moved. The two girls huddled closer together, terrified of what might happen next.

But the only thing that came through the gap was a sliver of moonlight. It shone on Ellie's backpack where she had dropped it, just inside the entrance.

Then the backpack began to move.

Chapter 10

Ellie stared in amazement as her backpack slid slowly out of the tent. What on earth would a wolf want with a backpack?

She tugged on Kate's arm and pointed toward the entrance. In the dim light of the moon, she saw her friend nod and start to crawl silently out of her sleeping bag. Ellie did the same. Very, very quietly, they crept forward and peered through the tent flap.

Their mystery visitor had its nose deep in the backpack.

"It's a deer," whispered Ellie in surprise. Although she spoke as quietly as she could, her voice was loud enough to startle the animal. He pulled his head out of the backpack and stared at them in alarm.

His antlers looked magnificent silhouetted against the moonlit sky, but the image was spoiled by one of Ellie's socks, which was dangling from his mouth.

The two friends stayed so still that they hardly even dared to breathe. It was wonderful to be that close to a wild deer. They didn't want to scare him away.

At that moment, there was a new sound, coming from behind the tent. It wasn't the quiet padding of paws, or the light tread of another deer. This was the unmistakable thud of hooves.

Ellie's heart sank as she saw Moonbeam wander into sight. The palomino had escaped again, and she had chosen exactly the wrong moment to come searching for more cereal.

But the deer didn't run away. Instead, he turned his head to look at Moonbeam, and, for the first time, Ellie noticed that his left ear drooped sideways.

The two girls looked at each other and simultaneously mouthed the word *Stanley*.

He wasn't a fawn anymore. He was a full-grown stag. But Kate's grandfather had been right. Stanley definitely wasn't as timid as most other deer. He stood completely still as

Moonbeam walked up to him. Then he dropped the sock, and each sniffed the other's nose.

The presence of another animal seemed to give Stanley extra confidence. He turned his attention to the backpack again. This time he had help. Moonbeam nuzzled it, too.

"What are they after?" asked Kate in a low voice.

"I bet it's my peppermints," Ellie whispered back. She reached into her jacket pocket and pulled out another pack. She crept out of the tent, holding out some peppermints in the palm of her hand.

She was too excited to care that her feet were bare and the grass damp with dew.

Stanley stepped back as Ellie came toward him. He kept close to Moonbeam's side, though his nose twitched as he smelled the scent of peppermint. So did Moonbeam's. The palomino reached out and took the sweet as soon as Ellie was close enough.

Ellie tossed another one to Stanley. It landed just in front of him, and he ate it up happily. Then he came forward, looking for more. Kate gave him the next one. She tossed it on the ground beside the tent.

As the deer bent his head to reach the mint, one of his antlers touched the pink material. It made a familiar scratching sound—one that Ellie remembered from the night before. "So it wasn't claws at all," she said.

"But I don't blame you for thinking it was," Kate replied with a grin. Then she glanced at her watch. "It's midnight. Just the right time for a snack."

They spread blankets on the damp grass and wrapped themselves in their sleeping bags. Then they sat outside in the moonlight and munched on chocolate cake and potato chips.

Moonbeam and Stanley grazed happily beside the girls. Above them, thousands of stars twinkled in the velvety sky.

Ellie reached into her pocket again and pulled out the cell phone. "I don't need this," she said, tossing it inside the tent. She felt happy there, with Kate, and the ponies, and Stanley. The King had been completely wrong. Camping really was fun.

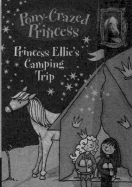
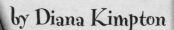